4.98

D1377884

GARDNER-WEBB COLLEGE LIBRARY
P. O. Box 836
Bolling Springs, N.C. 28017

THE GREAT APE

THE GREAT APE

*BEING THE TRUE VERSION OF THE FAMOUS SAGA OF
ADVENTURE AND FRIENDSHIP NEWLY DISCOVERED
BY FERNANDO KRAHN*

The Viking Press, *New York* / Kestrel Books, *London*

GARDNER-WEBB COLLEGE LIBRARY
P. O. Box 836
Boiling Springs, N.C. 28017

child. Lt.
PZ
7
.K8585
Gr

THE VIKING PRESS
625 Madison Avenue, New York, N.Y. 10022
KESTREL BOOKS
Published by Penguin Books, Ltd., Harmondsworth, Middlesex, England
Copyright © 1978 by Fernando Krahn
All rights reserved. No part of this publication may be reproduced,
stored in a retrieval system, or transmitted in any form or by any means,
electronic, mechanical, photocopying, recording, or otherwise, without the prior
permission of the Copyright owner.
Published in 1978 by The Viking Press and Kestrel Books
Published simultaneously in Canada by Penguin Books Canada Limited
Printed in the United States of America
1   2   3   4   5   82   81   80   79   78

Library of Congress Cataloging in Publication Data
Krahn, Fernando. The great ape.
Summary: A little girl meets an extraordinarily
large ape on a tropical island.
[1. Apes—Fiction.   2. Friendship—Fiction.
3. Stories without words.]   I. Title.
PZ7.K8585Gr   [E]   78-9053
ISBN 0-670-34840-6 (United States of America)
ISBN 0-7226-5519-3 (Great Britain)

GARDNER-WEBB COLLEGE LIBRARY
P. O. Box 836
Bolling Springs, N.C. 28017

Child. Lit.
PZ
7   Krahn, Fernando
          The great ape
.K8585
Gr